Caught Between Two Worlds

Caught Between Two Worlds

Gail Cheatam

Copyright

Caught Between Two Worlds is a work of fiction. The names, characters, businesses, places, events, incidents and dialogue are drawn from the author's imagination and are not to be construed as real. Any resemblance to actual events or persons, living or dead, is entirely coincidental.

Printed in the United States of America.
First Printing, 2017

ISBN-13: 978-1-947656-04-8
ISBN10: 194765604x

The Butterfly Typeface Publishing
PO BOX 56193
Little Rock Arkansas 72215

Dedication

Caught Between Two Worlds is dedicated to my family who always believed. It is especially dedicated to my brother Ray Earl Fluker (01/31/1964 – 03/13/2015) who fought with love audaciously a dreadful war that finally drew him to death. Forever, my soul weeps for the tenderness of your voice, your unspoken dialogue, your soft kiss, your kind smile, your gentle embrace; your genuine "I love you".

"Never be limited by other people limited imaginations. If you adopt their attitudes, then the possibility won't exist because you'll have already shut it out...You can hear other people's wisdom, but you've got to re-evaluate the world for yourself."

– Mae Jemison

Table of Contents

Acknowledgments

When I learned, Iris M. Williams of *Butterfly Typeface Publishing* expressed an interest in publishing my book *"Caught Between Two Worlds,"* I stood in awe and disbelief. I was anxiously excited about all the possibilities of being a published author. After many and long discussions, I felt drawn to trust Iris to help me bring to fruition my precious baby, my first novel. As our trust was strengthened around challenges of time and restraints, I learned that moreover, we are connected through time, place and familiar. It is with these circumstances, I surrendered to Iris the publishing of *"Caught Between Two Worlds"*.

For my parents: Your place in my journey can never be questioned, you are first!

Odell Cheatam: In many ways, you endured great peaks and valleys in order for me to hold a place in this history. Like your mother, Annie M. Cheatam, your greatest teaching for love and family is nothing less than remarkable. Similar to Jackson's struggles, you have fought great battles for your family's survival. You bring incredible balance and height into my life. I am humbled by your dedication, patience, encouragements and love to make sure I achieve my writing ambitions. Your commitment to me has influenced our children and grandchildren to go beyond the invisible and visible line - the unknown.

Danielle: Your natural talents are unsung and your contextual insight is impeccable.

Evelyn: I am grateful for your daring and influential firmness. Your level of discipline is absolutely amazing and was much needed.

Paretta *(Sonya)*: Your courageous gift of laughter and determination fuels me to do better. Anything I attempt to do, trial or failure, you treat it with profound greatness. Your *"You know I got you mama"* motto catapults me to not only explore every gift, but to accept the challenge of the unknowingness of those gifts. Likewise, and very similar to my first novel, you are my first born.

LaShonda: Your strong-suit, your candidacy and spicy diplomacy, are the very fabrics of your internal magnificence and it intertwines with my soul. Your determination took you above the familiar compliancy; thus, it landed you in a place of continuity. Like Jackson, in a world where gifts and talents are overshadowed by blindness, your raw purpose of life is yet to be discovered.

Antawne *(the* song in my heart): "You are

my sunshine. My only sunshine. You make me happy when skies are grey..." You are my reason to live and the air I breathe. The challenges of you, born with Downs Syndrome, are my rock of lessons learned. We outlasted ignorance with the power of unconditional love.

I must give homage to my nieces: Ja'Tyia and Jami, whose genuine love for me read out loud, non-stop, the adventures of Jackson and his friends.

For my grandchildren and great-grand daughter, Samiiyah: I write to enlighten, to inspire and to validate a place for you. (LaShay, Kayla, Victoria, Nicholas and Nicole, Olivia, Cenea, Alexandria Rose, and a blessed gift, Czaria who is promised to arrive by February 2018.)

For my extended family and friends: Because you "know me Love" you have contributed to this body of work and to the life of Gail Cheatam!

Prelude

Boys and Girls

Almost anyone will agree that boys can make life interesting! They manage to find endless activities to occupy themselves. These activities may range from playing constructive sports to simply running and tossing a football in a park or being mischievous to girls. Many boys like to play rough, tease other kids or hang with their friends.

Then, there are boys who are destined to overcome challenges and are driven to choose between right and wrong. While the role of boys can be taxing, girls are sometime just as rambunctious and interesting. Girls who try to do what boys do may not always be as interesting, resourceful or mischievous. When it comes to such activities as athleticism, they can be just as competitive as boys.

Both boys and girls have one common similarity, codes. They are aware of the unspoken playground rules. The rule implies that boys and girls think it is *okay* for boys to taunt boys, but it's not all right for boys to taunt girls or girls to taunt girls. Overall, kids think that those playground antics are merely about children teasing and playing with each other.

For Jackson there were no exceptions to the rule. With a reputation as the toughest kid in middle school, Jackson could tease anybody he felt like messing with anytime he felt like it. In the same manner, if a girl hit him he'd hit her back, because some of them hit as hard as a dude. If a boy hit him he gladly returned a harder blow, to set an example for others. For this reason, most of the kids at Jackson's middle school feared him. To tell the truth, most of the teachers avoided him as well. His size, quiet demeanor and unpredictable sarcasm intimidated them.

However, underneath the tough skin, Jackson was a gentle giant. He was thoughtful and quiet spoken until the giant in him was awakened. As the tallest kid in middle school by age fourteen, Jackson towered over classmates like city buildings over sidewalks. His long arms extended past his thick torso to his mid-thighs. His open hands could easily match the size of a dinner plate.

Already, he wore size fifteen and a half shoes. His mom jokingly complained that his shoes cost as much as a summer month's electrical bill. Sometimes she teased him saying,

"Boy, if those feet of yours get any bigger, I'll have to use 'em to hold candles."

In elementary school, kids teased Jackson a lot about his weight and the amount of food he ate. In the beginning it did not bother him because he believed they were his friends. Then one day during lunch, he noticed some kids mocking him. He was trying to stuff two hot dogs and potato chips in his mouth when he overheard someone whispering bad things about how he was eating.

"He eats like a fat pig," ridiculed a girl.

"Only a pig can eat like that," another kid stated.

Other kids laughed and made pig noises. He saw kids rubbing their noses into their hands while pretending to eat like pigs from a trough. Jackson was terribly disappointed with them, but more so with himself. He realized they were not his friends. From that point on, Jackson decided to stop eating lunch with them, because he no longer felt safe or comfortable.

Chapter One

Instincts and Contradictions

Jackson's first instinct was to hide by skipping class. He had gotten into trouble, multiple times over hiding out in an empty classroom. Once, he was caught sleeping in a custodial closet. The escapes were places of respite for him. It provided a place of solitude for him to get away from the hatred inflicted on him by rude, annoying kids. Moreover, it helped him to get away from his fears and thoughts of responding violently toward them.

Skipping classes threatened to get him suspended from school so Jackson would often arrive to class seconds before the tardy bell rang just to avoid the kids' rude stares and savage behaviors. He'd make a straight line to the back of the classroom, sat in the last chair and lay his head on the desk pretending to sleep. Jackson knew he had a physical advantage over any one of them but refused to use his strength to retaliate against them despite the way they treated him.

Somewhere between fifth and sixth grade Jackson grew even taller and gained a few more pounds. He expected middle school to be different than elementary school and it was; children who had teased him in elementary school avoided him completely in middle school. From the corner of his eye, Jackson saw them looking at him and they realized he saw them, they quickly looked in another direction. He knew they remembered the terrible, awful things they did to him. Like Jackson, the on-lookers hoped he didn't remember how badly they had treated him. Other children avoided him altogether because of negative rumors that followed him as well as his size.

Jackson did remember how badly his peers had mistreated him in elementary school. He remembered the mean, degrading and hateful things they said to him. Shamefully, Jackson remembered the disappointment and hurt he felt. He also recalled hiding out in empty rooms, sobbing like a baby and then complaining to his parents about how awful the kids were toward him.

Sadly though, his dad failed to understand or accept how Jackson felt. As such, his dad did not encourage his pity, even telling him to, "Suck-it up Junior. You're not a baby anymore. You're a big boy now. Show no fear or kids will think you're just a big punk. Ain't nobody gon' respect a punk! You got to stand up to 'em, Junior," he labored in a forceful tone.

When teachers and coaches, especially the "organized" sports coaches, approached Jackson, they all seem to see one thing, a professional athlete. Jackson had the physical build to be a solid basketball, football player or play any major sport. Some of the coaches, talking amongst themselves, saw him as a golden ticket to jump start or revive their stale career status. In their small but equal minds, a mere probability of Jackson's potential meant media recognition, big dollars for the athletic department, the school and for some, personal career advancement.

Contrary to their stereotypical thinking, Jackson did not like sports, none of them - basketball, football, baseball, golf, wrestling, not even track and field. Swimming was definitely out of the question because he had never learned how to swim. He was tired of teachers, students and coaches constantly asking, "Who's your favorite team? What team you going to play for?"

Even people in the community repeatedly asked him the same annoying questions, "Hey son, what basketball team you gon' play for? What position you pressing for, power forward or center?"

Jackson realized these people were excited for him. He understood that they were proud to be acquainted with his *possible* life-changing potential. Some even wanted to believe that they had somehow contributed to his life.

However, Jackson grew weary of people equating his physical stature and the color of his skin with sports. He hated when they asked him questions about sports, as if they thought he didn't know how to do anything else or was incapable of learning how to do anything else. Even worse, when he told them he didn't have any interest in sports, their disappointed facial expressions left an uncomfortable feeling below his rib bones.

"What a waste of size and potential talent. That's a darn shame," some would say.

The harsh comments made Jackson feel hurt and lonely. "A boy your size could be the next superstar," they continued, shaking their heads in disgust and dismissing him altogether.

Most of the critics never even asked Jackson what he liked or what he wanted to do when he grew up. As if that wasn't enough, he also had to deal with the hardcore rebels who did not hesitate to use strong, choice vernacular, warning him of what they would do if he was their son. In an unspoken manner, Jackson's 'rude' rejection to their concerns about his future, spoke to a much deeper, personal loss for those in his community. His detached reaction was seen as a much bigger issue than Jackson could possibly understand. His seemingly ungrateful attitude spoke against a disenfranchised culture whose forefathers fought long and hard and died so children like him could have a better chance in life. It was the worst form of oppressive setback.

The people didn't hesitate to voice their disappointment in seeing such physical ability go to waste along with the potential opportunity for a free college education. Others responded bitterly, as they believed he had no right, at his age, to turn down an opportunity to escape deprivation. Moreover, to deny his parents an opportunity for a better lifestyle was outright selfish. Yet, the only way they could seriously justify or excuse such loss and disappointment was to think that he was a big, dumb, clumsy kid and that his parents were being irresponsible. How else could they justify the selfish disregard for a better lifestyle for him and his family?

In his young mind, Jackson figured, the sports professions were overrated. It set many kids up with false hope or gave them the wrong impression about what it truly meant to become a professional athlete. Some children weren't allowed or given the chance to think about abilities outside of sports. Jackson felt fairly certain that he had other talents just as reliable as basketball or football skills. Joining the football team or the basketball team, was pretty simple by comparison, he resolved. Players who showed up for daily practices and stayed motivated made the team.

There were two kinds of athletes, wannabe athletes and aspiring athletes. The overzealous, wannabe athletes thought talking-the-talk, watching Monday night games, or knowing their favorite athletes' statistics somehow gave them a physical advantage to becoming the next super-star athlete. For some, "a bench warmer" position was an achieved accolade.

The coaches' biggest challenges with these kids were to make them team players. Once they were released on the basketball court or football field, they often played independent of other team members. The wannabe athletes didn't do much to prepare their bodies or minds, Jackson thought. They didn't practice on their own or after school with the aspiring athletes, only when told to do so and even then, they didn't push harder to reach their full potential.

These same students thought they were superstars already and didn't feel the need to exercise as much. They had poor attitudes and many had bad grades. Well, maybe a few had pretty good grades, but if you put them on a basketball court or on a football field they suddenly thought they were gifted with super athletic abilities to play sports. It was like they woke up and thought they were the next Kobe Bryant, Magic Johnson, Larry Bird, Peyton Manning, or Tom Brady. Any fool or idiot could have figured it took practice and determination. Those guys worked hard in season and out of season to become the best of the best in their profession. Wannabe athletes did not.

Jackson had once asked his dad for advice about following one's dreams. His dad told him, "If you want something bad enough nobody has to force you to work at it."

Jackson remembered a kid named Ethan Edwards, a ninth-grader who always bragged about being a future running back for the Dallas

Cowboys. The kids at school hyped him up telling him he could be the next Joe Delaney, but all they knew about Joe was his stats. If you asked them anything else about Joe or how he died, they didn't know he drowned heroically trying to save the lives of three kids. Would they willingly put *their* lives at risk, like Joe Delaney, to save the life of another person? Everybody knew they were fake, scared punks with a lot of talk and nothing to back it up.

Ethan was barely five feet tall, bow-legged, weighed close to a hundred and five pounds soaking wet, even wearing his football uniform, pads and spiked shoes. He was always smiling, had curly brown hair, wore the latest fashions and the girls were mesmerized by him. He could hardly read, but he *could* definitely talk the talk. His teammates purposely argued with him because he always thought he knew more about sports than anyone else.

Jackson watched how some of the teammates intentionally ran into Ethan and knocked him to the ground just for the heck of it. They would snatch Ethan up from the ground with one hand, and propel him forward like a rag doll because he was so lightweight. The idiot coaches encouraging him to play knew Ethan was on an ego trip and would never make pro anything, except maybe in a sales job. A couple years later, Ethan was on the field running against a rival team, when an opposing player hit him. The impact was so hard it knocked Ethan unconscious, causing minor, temporary brain injury. Interestingly, Ethan landed about a foot from the goal line. Unfortunately for Ethan, he was banned from playing any contact sport from that time on.

Chapter Two

Inherited Talent

To Jackson's knowledge, there had never been any athletes in their family. It definitely wasn't on his radar to become the first one. He had his reputation and he liked it just the same. As long as the kids thought he was a tough guy, he was cool with the perceptual image. In any case he wasn't worried about anybody knocking him to the ground for the heck of it. Even though he looked like a jock, what Jackson wanted to do was far from being an athlete.

Although Jackson portrayed the role of a tough guy at school, at home he was very different. He enjoyed their family reunions, Fourth of July barbeques, birthday parties and Memorial Day gatherings where he could watch other people be lively and have fun.

Jackson's idea of relaxing was, listening to jazz musicians like Fats Domino, Duke Ellington, Ramsey Lewis, and Herbie Hancock. He loved Oscar Peterson. He admired iconic, music superstars like Stevie Wonder, Ray Charles and Axel Rose in their struggle to create dynamic music. If Alicia Keys was his age Jackson swore he would ask her to marry him. There were many other musicians he enjoyed just as much.

He wanted badly to share his excitement with his friends. However, sharing his interest was not something he felt comfortable telling them. He suspected they would not understand or that they were too immature to appreciate his passion and taste for music. The few times Jackson thought about telling his friends, he quickly dismissed the idea due to nervousness, and decided it wasn't the right time. He imagined his friends would ask lots of weird questions, same as the teachers and coaches or the people in his community. He couldn't bear to see the same look of disappointment on the faces of his friends. So, he resolved it would be best to keep his love for music to himself.

Over time Jackson learned to spend very little time with people who asked questions directly related to his stature and sports. The approach became a defense mechanism to help ward-off uncomfortable feelings in the bottom of his stomach. He had grown to dislike entertaining grown people's stupidity.

Inspired by his father and grandfather's history of playing in prominent jazz bands,

Jackson had a broad appetite for contemporary and classical music. His grandparents would have declared he was born with an old spirit and that Jackson had been here before. Everyone who heard Jackson play agreed he was born with an exceptional gift for music.

Deep down in his soul Jackson knew he had a calling to do something special. His number one interest was to become a famous pianist and music composer. Something inside of Jackson craved music all the time. He dreamed of a time when he could create musical masterpieces like his icons. Jackson was intrigued with the unique blends and balance of instrumental music. It mesmerized him the way musicians' blended instruments together to create something perfect. Jackson could have easily asked the music or band teachers for help with his passion for music, but he feared making a spectacle of himself.

The piano stood out most to Jackson. He visualized his fingers toying and dancing across the black and white keys producing wonderful, eclectic sounds. The diverse pitches and sounds teased his flesh raising the hairs on his arms. Jackson's thoughts of playing the piano proved a temporary fix for his musical craving. The piano was the one instrument capable of replicating different notes and sound pitches with its many keys. Like summer heat on a long hot day, the sounds that resonated from the piano lingered in his mind long after he experienced the notes. Of all the musical instruments, the piano by far was a mystical and, intriguing instrument for him to play. An experience that was no less hypnotic.

"The piano has eighty-eight keys," Jackson boasted, "fifty-two white keys and thirty-six black keys with a huge, flawless frequency range." For most of his young life, he watched and imitated modern day-musicians playing the piano. He had an ear for hearing the highly complex notes diverse classical songwriters played on the piano. After listening to the songs, he could instinctively replay it from memory on almost any instrument, most notably the piano.

Jackson recalled when he made his first piano. At age three, he had drawn wobbly black and white lines on top of one of his momma's shoeboxes. He was proud of the drawing because it made his mother cry happy tears. When she saw what he had done, she kneeled down in front of him, proudly held his little delicate-shoulders in her hands, looked into his eyes with a smile and said to him, "Junior, it is beautiful. Your piano reminds me so much of how much your grandpa loved and respected instrumental jazz." Then she hugged him saying, "I believe you'll become a famous pianist, like your great-grand daddy 'nem.

Those ole' men were mean piano players".

Still to this day, she liked teasing him about the homemade piano. Aside from the smile on her face, which made him smile, the drawing reminded him of how long he had enjoyed listening to music. As far back as he could remember, music of some sort had been a part of his life.

The many variations of distinctive sounds continued to intrigue his creative imagination. The sounds he heard were much more intrinsic than most people could imagine. The musical notes magically rang against his eardrums causing exciting, dramatic sensations. Inside his head, it felt like little miniature people were always mixing spellbinding melodies and rhythms that pulsated fine nerves between his ears. It was nothing short of remarkable to hear and taste music notes at such distinguishable pitches. He mildly compared his experience to the listeners of the famous "Drummer Boy" sermon, preached by Dr. Martin Luther King, Junior which Jackson had read repeatedly. In the same manner as the spiritual beats rang true in the hearts of people who heard the sermon, the piano tones uplifted his spirit.

Chapter Three

A Vivid Dream

Jackson arrived home early from school. The apartment was temporarily free of noise, chaos, and the stench of his father's drunkenness. Except for the stale odor of Newport cigarette smoke, the apartment felt safe and inviting. He slouched lazily on the well-used brown and burgundy plaid colored sofa that sat across the room from the muted Sanyo television.

Since his father lost his job, Jackson hardly ever had the apartment to himself anymore. He appreciated the quiet time to process the on-going turbulence in his young, restless mind.

Lately, Jackson's heart had been heavily burdened with confusion. It was more like he was being pulled between two worlds; one swayed with misguided beliefs taught by his parents and the other filled with a nagging, unfamiliar, but sweet and encouraging force that made him want to do something exciting, creative and risky.

What is wrong with me? Why do I feel this way? Jackson questioned himself.

Jackson stretched out his long body on the sofa propping one foot across the armrest. He shifted his body to avoid smelling the unpleasant cigarette odor. The sofa bottom caved in under his weight causing him to slouch deeper into the sofa back. Meanwhile his legs lay uncomfortably across the armrest. Each time he moved on the sofa, the unpleasant odor of musty cigarette smoke came through the wool fabric. He thought the odor was much stronger than the usual stench of day-old cigarette butts his father let pile-up in the ashtrays.

Jackson closed his eyes, placed one arm behind his head resting the other arm across his upper stomach. For the first time the bad-boy image felt illusive and marginal. He contemplated his options -- continue to be a fake, bad boy or tell his friends about his interest and talents in music. He wanted badly for his friends to know about his interest. Moreover, he wanted them to accept him.

But would they accept me or would they react like the superficial people who think I should play sports? He questioned sadly. *My friends know I'm in band class, but they have no idea just how much I enjoy it or how clever I am on the piano,"* he thought.

Unexpectedly, his mind drifted.   He felt weightless, falling into what seemed to be a never-ending darkness of entangling thoughts. Jackson landed on the bottom floor of soft darkness. He observed himself engaging in a deep, defensive discussion with his friends. He was explaining to them that although he never played solo, he somehow knew how to play different musical instruments. He told them how he played in the middle school jazz band and in elementary school when he was in fifth grade. Jackson continued to explain that he had never been taught to read music or play an instrument. He could listen and then played by ear.

He observed an unknown figure standing nearby that looked like an older version of himself. The unknown figure said, "Listen to him, he is right.   Jackson's gifted ability comes to him as simple as tying his shoes." He noticed his friends never responded to him or the unknown figure that defended him.

Jackson, repositioned himself to get more comfortable on the sofa wondering how all of this could be possible. To some degree, Jackson was mildly aware of his father, grandfather and other relatives' extensive involvement in music. However, he did not make the connection with himself. Somehow, he thought, I have to let my friends know about my interest in music.

Jackson drifted off into a quiet, thoughtful sleep wondering how his passion for music might change the way others saw him. He thought about how it might also bring his parents closer together.

What would my daddy think of me? He pondered silently. *How can I prove to everyone that my musical talents are just as good as any of the athletes running around with a ball on a basketball court or football field?*

Jackson's voice was faint as he whispered, "Perhaps my friends and kids at school will see me as the talented musician I really am and not some big bully. I don't want the kids at school to think of me as a bully anymore."

Jackson burrowed his body further into the smoke-scented sofa, falling into a deeper sleep. Strong, colorful childhood memories flooded his mind. In a dream, he relived everything, his actions, responses, everything.

The vivid dream made his past feel real and participatory. The details of the day Jackson stood in his fifth-grade classroom talking to the music teacher had remained dormant and stale in his mind, until now. Jackson was reliving his past life through the dream. He could hear this woman talking to him, in the dream, which he thought was odd.

"Jackson," the fifth-grade music teacher said to him, "I expect you will be the world's next renowned pianist."

He didn't fully understand what the word "renowned" meant, but he certainly understood how what she said made him feel. He held that good feeling dear to his heart. Jackson stood boldly in front of the teacher, wearing a pair of tattered, khaki pants and a blue tee shirt. He was on-guard to defend his boyhood. Thinking about what his father might say to him, he spoke with confidence to warn the music teacher, he would never amount to nothing but being a thug. "This country ain't ready for a real black man like me," he stated fluently.

At the time, little did he know her prediction for him would become the foundation for his musical path. The happiness he felt and the excitement he saw on his teacher's face humbled him inside.

His oversized body shifted from an uncomfortable position to a more reclined position. Jackson regained some awareness. Feeling bothered, yet baffled by the meaning of the dream, he wanted more. The post-dreamy state caused him to remain quiet and still on the sofa. Reminiscing through the past felt weird to him, but it also suggested he was on to something. For one, the dream might be a connection to untangling the endless thoughts.

It was still difficult for Jackson to believe the music teacher suggested, he could be someone special in music. As he lay motionless in a lethargic state, his eyes slowly closed and the memories of that day came alive.

The music teacher, Ms. Bell, frowned and tried to persuade Jackson to not be so eager to let those words flow from his mouth again.

It was sad, she thought. *He's blessed with genuine musical abilities and here he is believing he's going to be a thug.*

At the same time, Ms. Bell felt mortified with his parents for allowing him to think such a thing. She hoped to reason with him, as his talents were too important to his future.

"Jackson, I know you don't really believe what you are saying. So I am going to pretend I didn't hear you respond with such bitter vulgarity."

Jackson, unclear of Ms. Bell's comment, rolled his eyes thinking she misunderstood him. He felt bad about attacking Ms. Bell for saying such nice things about him and about his musical ability. He knew he didn't have any reason to doubt what Ms. Bell said to him, but his father's advice ruled his world.

Surely she wouldn't say I'm a genius if it wasn't true, he argued quietly to himself. *But why would my daddy say I'm gonna be a thug?*

His body reacted to the dream. He shifted into another uncomfortable position and finally woke up, once again puzzled by the dream because it felt real. He remained on the sofa mindful of his fifth-grade teacher's words and what they might have to do with his recent confusion.

Jackson weighed his options carefully. His father's macho teaching compared to the music teacher's nice comments, bothered him. Jackson had been duly warned though. His daddy dictated to him what a boy needed to do to prove himself to be a man. In his heart of hearts, Jackson wanted to be the man his daddy wanted him to be. However, inside of him a raging war took place and he didn't know how to bring peace to such internal turbulence.

"You are talented and smart," Ms. Bell encouraged him. "You are different, Jackson. If I had a tiny ounce of the talent you have shown in music, I might not be a music teacher today. I would have gladly traveled the world over-and-over singing and dancing to the lovely ballads of jazz music." She stared into a space past the classroom ceiling, placing her right hand over her full bosom as to cover shame for not following her passion for music.

An astounding voice pitched somewhere between Josephine Baker and Ella Fitzgerald replaced the air in the classroom. She sang a short ballad from one of Ella Fitzgerald's songs, which was unfamiliar to Jackson. Nonetheless, he could not escape the vehement splendor rising from her full, round belly and out through her mouth. It was the most beautiful sound, trapped, inside a human body he had ever heard. Her singing outshined his mother's Sunday morning imitation of Aretha Franklin's old spiritual hymns.

Jackson could not relate to the song Ms. Bell sang or to the struggle she sang about. Nor did he understand why she used big words like *"renowned* and *vulgarity."*

"What do they mean?" he questioned immaturely.

Like his father's man talk, Ms. Bell further confused him when she cleverly danced several improvisations of the waltz, while she sang. The strangeness choked his mind, leaving him totally confused about his father's motives and Ms. Bell's behavior.

"You don't know my daddy Ms. Bell," he asserted. "He will kill me if he knew I was talking to you about music and stuff."

"But why, Jackson?" she asked. "Surely he knows how talented you are, doesn't he?"

She stepped slightly away from his raised eyes hoping to give him time to think about what she asked him. Instead Jackson's eyes rolled up toward the ceiling and back to her face. Her lack of understanding exhausted him.

It ain't no use trying to explain nothing to her, he thought. Jackson decided, all his efforts were useless when trying to get Ms. Bell to understand what he was talking about.

In an innocent, unassuming eleven-year-old voice, Jackson repeated the words of his father, "How could a woman know what it feels like to be a black man?"

"I got to go home Ms. Bell," he said in a surly tone. "Please don't tell my momma or my daddy you talked to me about this music stuff."

He picked up his notebook and pencil and, placed them in his oversized black and green backpack, hurrying out of the room to catch up with his friends.

"Jackson, wake up. It's time to get ready for school, baby," his mom announced softly over the smell of warm blueberry pancakes. He peered from underneath the blanket, surveyed the room to separate the dream from reality. He quickly got up from underneath the blanket his mom had covered him with while he was asleep. In no time, he had showered and dressed for school.

The fresh memories of Ms. Bell motivated him to take a stand. Caught between two worlds he felt helpless in terms of what he wanted to do in life. He wanted to feel like the man his daddy urged him to be, but his dad's advice spoke to a very different man -- someone who was a fighter, an aggressor, an independent thinker, someone who had confidence in himself. For now, he felt determined to turn a misguided situation into something wonderful. The big question now was HOW?

"Junior, your dad said for you to come straight home from school today," his mom said as she went back into the kitchen.

"Mom, please call me Jackson. All my friends do." He rolled his eyes until the white showed between the lids, and then grabbed his backpack and walked out the door. He was careful not to slam it too hard. He knew if he did, his mom would make him come back; and walk out the door without slamming it. Once outside the building, he switched his focus to Ms. Bell. He felt strongly that the dream was a warning for him to take action.

"I've got to talk to Ms. Bell today," he stated firmly.

Chapter Four

Parental Frustrations

After Jackson's visit with Ms. Bell, he ran out of the building as fast as he could to catch up with his walking buddies, Terrill, Javion and Larry. The four of them had been friends since they were about seven years old.

"What did ole' Ms. Bell want to talk to you about, Jackson, and why is she always smiling at you?" Javion probed his friend when he caught up with them. "She ain't never nice to us," he complained.

Terrill added, "I hate it when she talks to me. Her teeth always got that red lipstick on them.

Yuck?" He closed his eyes and shuddered his shoulders.

"Uh ... she was just telling me about my grades and how I need to work a little harder in her class. I told her all right, but she was acting like she didn't believe me. So I told her to stop messing with me befo' I tell my daddy she picking on me. Y'all know my daddy don't like nobody messing with me. I told her that, too. I think that's why she keeps smiling at me too, 'cause she don't want my daddy to beat her up for talking crazy to me," Jackson said wide-eyed. He knew they would never believe that *ole* Ms. Bell had believed that he was some kind of musical genius since fifth grade.

"Man, everybody knows your daddy crazy," said Javion. "I bet he was a bully just like you when he went to school, huh Jackson?" Javion thought for a moment and then asked, "Do you think your daddy would beat-up my step daddy? I can't stand that evil dude. He always arguing and fighting with my mom. I hate it when he makes her cry. I wish he would go back to where ever he came from. I get real mad when he hit my little brother for accidentally breaking my mom's stuff. My mom ain't never hit my little brother. Y'all know my little brother is nice. He likes to play with stuff and sometimes accidents happen, but he don't mean to break stuff. It's just the way he is. My momma said he kind of special and God gave him his own special set of wings. I can't wait until I get big like my big brother and run away".

Everyone else listened quietly while Javion went on.

"I'm gonna get a good job making lots of money and take my brother and my momma away from that fool! We'll see who he picks on then. That dude don't deserve us."

Jackson understood Javion's frustration about his stepdad's behavior. But he couldn't ask his dad to beat up Javion's stepdad any more than he wanted to correct him about being a bully or talk about his interest in music.

These isolated discussions were the opportune time to talk about whatever they wanted to talk about and nobody judge them. They didn't dare discuss their problems and concerns with anyone outside of their group. Likewise, they didn't discuss everything that went on in their homes, either. The conversations were reinforced by their parents' rule: What goes on in our home, stays in our home.

"Javion," Jackson said, "You can't be no punk. That's what my daddy tells me. My daddy gets mean with my momma too, but she'll fight that dude back. I get scared sometimes, but I go to my room and play my PS3 or listen to cool music on my iPod. I don't like it when my little sister gets scared and start crying though. I tell her to come in my room and watch me play games." Jackson looked over at his other friend. "What about you, Terrill?" asked Jackson. Terrill didn't answer. "What about you Terrill?" Jackson asked again.

The heavy discussion took them half way across the city park, which was named after Martin Luther King, Jr. Crossing the park was the shortest distance from school to their apartment buildings. The boys lived on the same block, but in separate buildings.

"My dad is cool most of the time," Terrill responded politely as he dropped his backpack onto the packed green grass near the walking path. He took out a football and ran backward. They tossed the football back and forth to each other several times. Then Terrill continued, "Sometimes, he tries to yell at my mom but she doesn't pay him any attention. My mom makes him a nice dinner and after dinner, he watches television until he falls asleep."

They enjoyed walking across the park, because it made them feel like big boys, as they would soon be going to high school. When crossing the park, they saw high school boys and girls kissing and messing around after school. They also saw other stuff going on in the park, like people fighting, homeless people sleeping on park benches and people shooting dice, among other weird things. One time they watched two police officers chase a naked guy across the park. The man was laughing loudly, ducking in and out of bushes to get away from the police officers. It was obvious the man was familiar with the park's hiding places because he kept getting away from the police officers. So, they knew crossing the park could be dangerous.

Chapter Five

Big Boy Parks

"Hey li'l man, what y'all doing in my park?" an oversized boy questioned critically. His voice sounded heavy and intimidating.

Jackson thought the boy was too big to be a school kid. However, his face didn't look to be much older than theirs. The big boy's dark skin appeared scaly, ashy, and dull in color. He bravely sported a tattoo on his right arm, between his elbow and wrist, that read *"Thug Pain"* complete with some sort of crossed swords, a symbol of a red rose and dripping blood etched on the handle. On the left side of the boy's dark face, was a long, battle scar that disappeared underneath his chin. Jackson distinctly noted how the blades evenly pointed upward in a perfectly crossed position.

The big boy's eyes looked strange, tired and lifeless, as if they were sunken deep in their dark sockets. The hair on his head looked like that of a sheep's butt; rough, nappy, and unclean and his breath reeked of awful halitosis. His crooked, yellow stained teeth were double stacked and in need of serious dental repair. The big boy stared savagely into Jackson's fixed gaze.

With the evening sun abruptly setting behind them, the big boy's dark, rough skin around the facial scar turned a shade of blue-black. The big boy's body appeared even more enormous and burly blocking the last of the evening sun over them. The big boy's rough appearance and the ghastly scar benumbed the four young boys. Jackson and his friends felt trapped. They were too frightened to respond to the oversized boy's question. Jackson and Javion, stood closest to the boy, paralyzed by his dark complexion and rough skin. The bigness of his body parts further increased their fear of him.

"I said, wadda' y'all lookin' at?" the big boy demanded, hunching his shoulders and clinching his fist defensively. When none of them responded to his threatening behavior, the big boy repeated he question again with such force that the spit flew though his teeth barely missing Jackson's cheek.

Larry, a strong, athletically endowed runner, took off like the *"Roadrunner"* cartoon character, *boinging*, and leaping high off the padded grass. With swiftness, he rotated his feet. His legs moved so fast, it looked like he was kicking his own butt.

Jackson and Javion were the last to back away slowly. While keeping an eye on the big boy, Terrill moved strategically toward their backpacks. His intention, after he grabbed the backpacks, was to catch up with Larry, but by then Larry was almost out of sight.

"Hey, Larry... Man, wait up!" Terrill yelled at his backside. But, the air and distance between them prevented Larry from hearing Terrill yelling for him.

Larry was athletically endowed and light on his feet. He could outrun any of them. At five-feet-six inches tall, Larry was the fastest on the track and field team and had achieved many awards and trophies to show for it. His chestnut-brown complexion and auburn-red hair made him just as popular with the girls.

When Jackson, Javion and Terrill caught

up with Larry, he was home waiting for them. The boys were seriously out of breath and badly in need of water to moisten their dry throats. Larry, laughed heartedly, teasing them about running so slow. Jackson didn't take lightly to Larry's teasing them.

"Larry, why you run from the dude in the park?" Jackson asked arrogantly between short breaths. Suddenly, Jackson remembered his mom telling him to come straight home from school. He turned and walked away from Larry, not waiting for a response.

"I don't know," Larry spoke to Jackson's backside. "He looked scary to me. I...I just don't like strangers," Larry replied nervously to Terrill and Javion. "Did you see that ugly scar on his face?"

Javion threw the football to Larry. "Larry,"

Javion said, "you might be the fastest runner out all of us but you the biggest wimp," he laughed out loud! "I'll see ya'll tomorrow at the post. I gotta go. I promised my mom I would help her with my little brother tonight." Javion walked away shaking his head.

"Yeah, me too. I got to help my mom with dinner," Larry responded. They each threw up the peace sign. "Peace-out," they said in unison.

Javion walked up the steps timidly. Before he went into his apartment, he noticed Larry still sitting on the front stoop. He thought maybe Larry was just hanging out before going into the house. Javion opened the door to enter into his apartment. When he looked toward Larry again, he saw two boys riding up on candy red bicycles with shiny, silver trimming. He watched Larry walked down the steps greeting the boys with hi-fives.

Guess he know 'em, Javion thought.

But something inside Javion felt wrong and insecure.   At his age, most everything felt intrusively wrong for him. His grandmother, Nana, whom he confided, encouraged him not to worry and he would soon grow out of those feelings.

Too bad today is not it," he wavered. Javion went inside the apartment and closed the door behind him. He was still slightly concerned about the guys on the bicycles. Underneath his feelings were thoughts about the tattoo and scar on the big boy's arm.

Chapter Six

Grateful

The boys were grateful that school was almost over for the summer. Grateful too they would not have to cross MLK Park or see the ghastly, huge boy. He was there almost every day when they crossed the park. It didn't matter if they were going to school or going home. While he didn't say much to them, he would pop-up unexpectedly from behind a tree or a large bush, mugging or ridiculing them.

"Hey, don't y'all have a home to go to? Why y'all keep comin' through my park, walkin' on my grass?" he would ask hatefully. "This is my park and you punks better stop comin' 'through here," he warned, grinning like a crazy fool. The boys didn't take kindly to his threats and the big boy's mischievous behavior had become more than a nuisance to Jackson.

Because of the big boy's threatening demeanor, Jackson and his friends rarely stopped anymore to toss the football or play in the park. They were at their wits' end with the big boy's bullying and threatening behavior. They had grown tired of him jumping out of bushes and making degrading remarks toward them when they crossed the park. Collectively they were angry with the idea that the boy's bullying behavior prohibited them from playing freely in the park. Their fears of him pushed them into action. They strategized a plan on the best ways to retaliate or to defend themselves, if he tried anything with them.

It was easy for them to ridicule the boy's

bigness, his dark complexion, scruffy appearance, scaly skin and big feet. However, they were not mentally prepared to tackle the boy physically. Nor were they prepared to cause him bodily harm.

Jackson didn't like belittling the big boy because he knew what it felt like to be taunted. But, like his daddy always told him, "Show no fear or kids will think you're just a big punk. Ain't nobody gon' respect a punk! You got to stand up to 'em, Junior." His father's warning gave Jackson a false sense of power and it fueled his ego. Jackson encouraged his friends that they might have to take revenge, first. They were nervous about what they would do if the boy tried to attack them first. The more they planned their attack, the less fear they harbored against the boy.

Javion, Larry and Terrill wondered what to do if Jackson backed out, because they were depending on him and now, in the presence of the big boy, Jackson didn't seem so tough. *After all, the big boy* REALLY *is a bad boy,* they thought.

"He probably sleeps in the park and eats garbage," Jackson stated coldly. The others nodded their head agreeing with Jackson.

"I wish we could play in the park without him bothering us," Larry's face was crestfallen as he spoke.

"I don't want people thinking we're punks cause we're afraid of him." Terrill added.

"Hey, we could name him Big Boy Parks, Javion said laughing nervously. "He's big and he lives in the park," he explained.

"I really think we should tell our parents about him," Larry said to Jackson.

"What will that do, Larry? We ain't supposed to walk across the park anyway. Don't you remember? Our parents told us not to go in the park because of all the bad stuff that goes on."

"No. No. No!" Terrill interrupted, shaking his head quickly. "If we tell our parents they will put us on punishment. I can't get on punishment no more this month. Y'all know they'll make us walk through the neighborhood," he continued.

"I agree," Jackson said. "Terrill is right. It's no use telling our parents. They'll make us stop walking through the park. I don't know about y'all, but I don't like walking through these neighborhood streets to get home. They are too close to traffic," Jackson added. "And don't forget about Reggie and his gang. I don't feel comfortable taking the main street to get home. Remember the people they pushed in front of those cars? Listen up, y'all. We only have a few more days befo' school is out for summer. We can handle it for a little while longer. We boys, right?" Jackson demanded. "It's Tuesday, just three more days before the weekend. Friday is a half day." He said to Larry and Javion who were listening intently.

Despite the big boy's threats, they decided to walk across the park, for the rest of the week. Surprisingly, they had not seen the boy jumping out of the bushes lately. Thinking perhaps he no longer posed a threat, they stopped to toss the football around for a while. It felt good to spend time hanging out, just being boys, before going home. They shared a few laughs and stories about the latest happenings in their homes.

Jackson wanted to tell them about his interest in music but thought better of it. The only thing they had to be mindful of was getting home before the streetlights came on. Otherwise they would get into serious trouble. They all hoped Big Boy Parks would not be in the park on Friday's half-day dismissal, either.

Chapter Seven

Meeting Rylea

Javion was excited. He had earned forty dollars helping his grandmother with chores around the house. "I have a surprise for y'all when we meet after school," he announced happily.

Jackson was a little skeptical and jealous about Javion's plans. Since Jackson was used to making the group's decisions, he wanted to know the plans before everyone else. But he knew Javion was trustworthy enough to handle the others.

"I promise we'll all get home before dark. Like I said, I ain't trying to get on punishment," Javion said while jogging up the steps, in front of the school building.

The boys were quite sure they could count on Javion to do what he said he would do. Moreover, they were excited about doing anything outside of playing under duress in the park or hanging out in front of the apartment buildings.

Jackson caught up with Javion in the hallway. "What's the deal, Javion? What do you have up your sleeve for after school?"

Javion wouldn't budge. "It's a surprise," he said excitedly.

Jackson felt someone staring at his back. When he turned around he noticed a tall, beautiful, girl staring back at him. She smiled affectionately at him. He knew everyone in the eighth grade. How had he missed such a beauty? *Why haven't I noticed her before? She must be new at school*, he pondered nervously, as she moved toward him.

"Hi, I'm Rylea. What's your name?" the new girl asked warmly. She stood gallantly in his personal space, as if she didn't know any better. Her hand hung suspended in mid-air between them, as she waited for him to accept her friendly introduction.

Jackson, captivated by her beauty, said nothing. *Why's she talking to me? Everyone knows who I am.*

"Hello, my name is Rylea. "What's yours?" she asked again. When he still didn't respond, she clasped her sweaty hands together and rubbed them slightly before dropping them to her side. "I'm just trying to make some friends," she continued. "My mom and dad recently got a divorce. We moved here from Chicago, my little sister, my mom and me. I started school here two days ago. I'm sure you're thinking what crazy parent would move their children to a new school at the end of the school year? I thought the same thing, but you have to know my mom," she stated awkwardly. "It's the way my parents operate ... just up and relocate to a different state. We're used to moving on short notice. I'm a military brat. My dad was in the military long before I was born. I've lived in six different states since I was in third grade." Rylea paused, abruptly changing the conversation. "I saw you with your friends in the park a couple days ago. I walk through the park too. I get scared when I see that gigantic, hideous boy. You know, the one with the ugly scar on his face. I know you saw him too," she paused again. She shook her head. "Sorry," she said. "I tend to get carried away and ramble sometimes when I'm nervous or afraid about something."

The tardy bell rang for their fifth hour class. Jackson noticed she had a worried look in her eyes. He suddenly remembered he was supposed to meet the fellas behind the gym after school. *It probably wouldn't be a good idea to show up with a girl,* he said to himself.

"Uh, my name is Jackson," he said shyly.

Then he heard his teacher, Ms. Bell yelling, "Let's get to class students. You don't want to be late."

Jackson looked in Ms. Bell's direction and back at Rylea's pretty face. Her eyes would not allow him say "no" to her. "Can you meet me behind the gym after school? Some of my friends will be waiting there too," he whispered shyly.

"Yes, absolutely! Thank you, Jackson," she whispered back to him.

Like the sound of a beautiful piano melody

her tender voice lingered in his head as he walked into ole' Ms. Bell's music class. Most of the time he had a bad attitude by the time he got to her class but today he was very pleasant.

He felt good. Excited. The feeling resonated with those in the dream he's had the other day. Other girls had tried to get with him, but they had not made him feel happy. He would purposely say mean things to them just so they wouldn't come back to bother him. *Rylea...* Her name rolled off his tongue like the sweet flavor of Jolly Rancher green-apple candy.

Ms. Bell, being watchful, saw a mischievous grin on his face. "Mr. Jackson, are you excited about your upcoming summer vacation," she teased.

"Aw, Ms. Bell, you already know, we too poor to take a real vacation," he replied playfully as he placed his long body lazily in the too-small chair. Surprised by his entertaining response, she held the moment to ask him to help get class started.

"Jackson, will you do me the honor of getting us started today?" she instructed politely.

This was a moment Ms. Bell had long hoped to witness from Jackson. If her prediction was right, this moment could prove more important for him than for her - to know she was correct about his music ability.

"Yes ma'am," he replied energetically. Jackson welcomed the opportunity to help start the class. With a slight swag, he strolled up to the raised podium. He flipped through several pages of sheet music. Standing erect, eyes focused, he stared out into the sea of students and tapped two sharp, crisp clicks on the front edge of the podium.

Then, as if he were a conductor preparing his orchestra, he raised the baton with his left hand. His right hand mechanically sailed upward, cueing the students to practice their first course notes.

He continued, directing each instrument group, page-by-page, through the practice notes. Once all the instruments had been tuned, he made a final practice tap on the edge of the podium bringing all instruments together in perfect harmony. He raised the baton again, cueing all band members to play in unison.

Ms. Bell, pretending not to pay attention to him, raised sheet-papers to her face to cover a huge grin. Jackson exceeded her expectations, as she was fondly surprised when he directed the groups flawlessly. Jackson could see her smiling as he looked to her for approval. The students were excited, pleased with a successful practice.

"They're ready for you." He gave Ms. Bell a quick head nod as he stepped down from the podium, smiling proudly. Hands clasped behind his back like a confident maestro, be leaned forward, bowing appreciatively for the audience recognition of his successful delivery. The students laughed softly at him for showing off.

They, clapped enthusiastically when he proceeded to take his place at the piano. Some asked Ms. Bell to let Jackson teach the class. "Perhaps another day," she responded warmly.

Ms. Bell was thoroughly impressed, as she observed his every move. From his confident swag to the podium, to the wrist flex in how he tapped the edge of the podium, to his attentiveness and listening skills, to his bending forward to thank the students for applauding, he had displayed such control. She saw how focused, yet distant he was in his sharp delivery, bringing the students to attention. He had turned the pages in the practice book, but he never once looked back at the practice pages. It was amazing for her to witness.

She felt humbled by the experience. In awe, she laid her right hand over her full bosom. She was proud to see him orchestrate the group with such audacity, authority and confidence. She peered straight through the ceiling, "Thank you, Lord," she stated gratefully.

Ms. Bell quietly thanked Jackson, letting him know she welcomed the attitude change. She hoped this experience motivated him to appreciate his raw talent. "I hope to see you just as happy at tomorrow's end-of-year musical performance and next school term too," she said with a smile.

"Yes ma'am," he said respectfully. While

responding to her, the fifth-grade discussion resonated in his mind, and danced throughout his thoughts.

Chapter Eight

Music Mastery

All the band and chorus members had quietly assembled in the gymnasium to practice the final performance selections.

The students were anxious but mostly excited to finish the performance. Meanwhile, Ms. Bell reminded the students about what they should wear to the final performance and behavior expectations.

"Students! Calm down. I know everyone is excited about our final performance. Let's go over the dress code and a few ground rules so you know what I expect." Ms. Bell clapped her hands several times together to get their attention, because of side talk. Once the nervous chatter subsided, she continued. "I expect everyone to dress properly for the occasion. Girls, please wear a black, knee-length dress with a nice pair of black shoes. Boys, you are to wear a long sleeve white shirt, black slacks and a black bowtie."

"Aw, Ms. Bell, you know we don't have no bowtie," one of the male students complained.

Ms. Bell nodded her head, "That's why I'm telling you now. Have an adult check out a thrift store or second-hand store. It's likely that you will be able to find a bowtie there." She raised both hands in the air. "Oh! And students, please remember to leave all electronic devices in the band room or with a family member. Make sure you take care of your personal needs like going to the restroom before you line up. As much as you can, do not talk during or in between sessions.

Pay close attention! And, absolutely no gum chewing!" she stated firmly.

Ms. Bell casually approached the podium. The students were conditioned to automatically come to full attention once Ms. Bell stepped onto the platform. Students sat upright, feet were flat on the floor and instruments were positioned for playing. She looked with pride at the many young, bright, talented faces. For a moment, her heart felt sorrow. She knew some would not return after summer and others would go on to high school. *Three years came and went too fast*, she thought as she singled out the eighth-grade students going to high school.

Then she collected herself, continued onto the platform and strolled up to the podium mic. Once again, she stood motionless, giving herself and each student any chance to make final adjustments. The students were ready, smiling and waiting eagerly to please her. They, along with Ms. Bell, had practiced hard and long for the school's final crescendo. The baton went up into the air. Her head nodded slightly toward them. All eyes and ears were like those of an animal locked on its prey. A clear, crisp, slap on the podium's edge cued them. The students raised their instruments and the tuning began.

Ms. Bell directed each group through the school's anthems. Then, she tapped the edge of the podium twice, with the baton, same as Jackson had done, cueing the students to the rhythmic beats of the music. As she listened to each instrument group, there was a very gentle, sweet replication of instrument pitches occurring between the instrument tuning. She redirected each individual instrument group to replay their part, hoping to hear the pitches duplicated again.

Then she ceased all the instruments to address the unfamiliar sound she had heard doing the warm-up.

"Students...students, everybody listen-up please," she instructed through the black stationary microphone. Ms. Bell peered over the top of a pair of silver-rimmed black reading glasses, narrowing her focus on students who were still prepping their instruments. "Look," she warned. "In order for us to get this right, you must follow my directions. Paying attention is crucial if we expect to present the school anthems perfectly for the end-of-year musical performance. We don't have a lot of time left to practice."

However, the mild, gentle pitches that were replicated did not escape her collective knowledge, musical experience or interpretation. While she didn't hear or couldn't easily identify an instrument replicating pitches, she recognized something authentic happening with one of her students' talents.

Ms. Bell was naturally intrigued by the student's ability to make pitch projections. Moreover, she was curious as to who could duplicate the instrument pitches with such mastery. Knowing how easily students could shut down if noted for doing something good, she hesitated on causing too much attention to the individual student.

She snapped her fingers together in conjunction with tapping the corner of the podium edge again. She cued multiple beats, intentionally listening to the clarinets, horns, guitars, etc. Then she raised the small, handheld marathon instrument to measure the tone, hoping to identify the instrument replication within the groups. The marathon displayed a very impeccable even tone scale masked between notes. With the length of the beats extended, she identified intonation coming from the piano. Her heart fluttered like a butterfly on a warm Savannah, Georgia day.

Impossible! Absolutely impossible, she silently declared. Every measurement on the marathon instrument confirmed the student at the piano displayed projective musical capability. She let the group continue to play in appreciation of the beautiful harmony coming from the piano keyboard. She observed Jackson's tightly-focused eyes. He appeared unconscious of duplicating notes. Ms. Bell marveled. *How can he blend the piano pitches so perfectly with other instrument groups?*

Jackson's body language was poised with intensity as he merged and imitated the delectable sounds of the other instruments. She could see him meticulously keying relative pitches and creating tone utterly similar to the other instruments currently being played. Jackson was producing the school's anthems in a very dramatic melody, making them sound like the other instruments. *What an incredible sense of music mastery,* she declared.

Knowing Jackson might not ever play the piece again, she wished she had recorded the practice. She debated whether or not to ask him if he was taking outside music lessons. She wanted to know who taught him to play the piano. *He can't possibly be taking lessons*, she mused, *He's always mentioned how poor they were.* She continued the practice until the students started complaining they were tired of playing the school anthems over and over again. The bell rang drawing their practice time to a close.

"Jackson, I'd like to see you for a moment please." The other kids clamored about putting away their instruments, preparing to leave the classroom. Jackson walked up to Ms. Bell at her podium.

"Yes, ma'am?" He asked with respect.

"Can you stay after school today?" Ms. Bell asked politely.

"No, Ma'am, I gotta' meet my momma right after school." He lied because he didn't want to be late meeting his friends behind the gym. He needed to get to the fellas before Rylea showed up.

"What about in the morning, before you go into the gym?" she asked. After seeing the satisfaction on Ms. Bell's face, he didn't want to disappoint her, like he did in elementary school.

"Yes ma'am. I'll try," he said while grabbing his music book, backpack and pencil off the floor. Jackson exited the room and rushed through the hallway to get outside.

Chapter Nine

The Giant Awakens

Once outside the school building, Jackson hustled to meet the fellas behind the gym. When he arrived, Rylea was the only one there waiting for him.

"Where's everybody?" he asked, staring at Rylea wearily. "We were supposed to meet behind the gym today. They're never late," he said.

Jackson was also buying time to. Being alone with Rylea was awkward and tense for him. He didn't know how to talk or react around a nice, pretty girl, especially one from Chicago. She had already proven to be different than the other girls at school.

"Where are they?" he whispered softly again. The palms of his hands were moist. Time slowed down to a morsel of a second. The sun raised its temperature making it warmer and brighter. Beads of sweat formed on his forehead, and more sweat rolled down the middle of his back. Underneath the navy-blue, poly-cotton tee shirt, his body felt wet and clammy. Perspiration under his armpits rolled down the side of his body.

While the area around him seemed to expand, the earth spun a tad bit faster. The usual screaming and laughter of children playing at the nearby playground quietly evaporated into the warm, clear atmosphere. Except for his irregular breathing and the abnormal thumps pounding behind his chest wall, his surroundings became quiet and distant. His stomach felt queasy.

"Are you okay?" Rylea asked. "You look like you're about to get sick. Your face looks flushed. Should I go try to find somebody to help you?"

Rylea watched his brown skin turn flushed like someone had painted him a pale brown color. The scowl on his face appeared out of place and strained. Jackson was nervously rubbing his hands together. She was concerned when he appeared shaky and detached. Just when she thought to ask him if he was okay again, she noticed a group of boys tossing a football near the football field.

"Are those your friends over by the football field? Maybe I could go ask some of them to help you."

"Oh yeah! Great," Jackson finally replied with transformed enthusiasm. "That's them!"

Knowing his friends were nearby energized him. Jackson was also relieved that he hadn't gotten their meeting place mixed up. If he had to walk Rylea home, *it would be a long walk*, he thought. *And what if I had to protect her from Big Boy Parks?* The thought chilled him. He smiled warmly at Rylea as she walked happily next to him.

Jackson liked girls. He just didn't like talking to them or being alone with them. He often felt shy and inadequate in the presence of a pretty girl. *Girls always seem much smarter. They know what to say, and can talk faster, without thinking about what to say next*, he thought. For him, he would think of something to say then forget the words coming from his brain through his mouth. Knowing Rylea was depending on him, he needed to act responsible and smart.

"Whoa! Jackson, who you got with you?" Terrill teased.

"Hey, everybody, this is Rylea," Jackson happily introduced her. "She walks across the park to get home too. She used to live in Chicago. She said she's kind of scared of the same big boy we saw in the park. I told her she could walk with us."

Rylea interjected. "We moved into the apartment building behind Jackson's apartment."

"It's cool," the boys said in rough unison. "We'll walk Rylea home first. Then we'll talk about going to the movie after school tomorrow. That's the surprise I mentioned to y'all," Javion said. "I've been saving my money from helping Nana with a few chores around the house. I think we even have enough money for popcorn, candy and soda!" He smiled. "We will have to hurry though if we want to get there during matinee time." The guys gave each other high-fives, laughing and bragging about the movies they wanted to see.

Before they knew it, they had entered the park. Javion noticed Rylea's personality changed abruptly. Her facial expression changed from a happy, pretty, smiling face to one of discontent and fear.

"Rylea, what's the problem? Are you afraid of Big Boy Parks? Your face looks sad all of a sudden. Aren't you ready to go home?" Javion asked with concern.

"I'm fine," she answered sharply. "After all, I'm with you guys. What could go wrong?"

Jackson, like Javion, was not convinced by her response because her body language implied something different. Although it was his first time meeting her, intuitively they could sense something was wrong. Jackson had had that same feeling around his mother, when she was upset or disappointed with his dad or him, more so with his dad for treating her mean.

Javion wanting to make her feel better asked, "Hey Rylea, how about the next time we go to the movies you ask your mom if you can go with us?"

"Okay. I will," she said, adding, "but I already know she'll tell me no. My parents are strict. They don't want me hanging out with, *'hoodlums',*" she said making quotation marks in the air with her fingers. She crossed her arms defensively and rolled her eyes. Then she said, "I know I sound ridiculous. Here you guys are going out of your way to help me get home safely and I'm calling you *'hoodlums'.*"

Larry chuckled a bit and shrugged his shoulders. "It's all good. I can relate to what you are going through Rylea. My parents are very strict as well. While I don't agree with everything they believe and all of their cultural norms and traditions, they hold true to their African culture and expect me to do the same. Maybe once your parents get to know us a little better, they will see that we're not *hoodlums* and trust us."

Terrill happily agreed, at the same time, wished that *he* had met Rylea first. "Yea, what Larry just said," Terrill stared at Rylea with his mouth open wide like he wanted to say more.

Jackson disliked the way Terrill stared into Rylea's face. He felt a certain kind of jealousy. He bumped Terrill in the back to get him to stop staring at her so brazenly. But, Jackson had to admit her beauty was nothing short of intoxicating.

The length of her soft, natural, almond-brown hair, long arms, petite waistline and gorgeous, long, skinny legs with a slight bow made her even more attractive. Her oversized marble like eyes looked like they had been dipped in pastel green paint, resting lazily under heavy lids demanding the boys' attention.

Rylea had a slanted smile that revealed a small gap between her teeth. Her high cheekbones and slender face were emphasized with cute, deep dimples. The color of her skin typically associated with Native American's complexion, was flawless. She was nothing short of a young, beautiful ivy plant waiting for full maturity. Everything about her was enticing. She was stunning.

Jackson shook his head. These feelings were unfamiliar to him. He disliked the way Terrill stared into the girl's face. *She's just a girl*, he mumbled to himself. Yes, she was pretty, but so were many other girls at his school. He didn't know what made Rylea take a front seat to the other girls, other than the fact that she made *him* feel good.

They walked deeper into the park, close to the place where Big Boy Parks normally showed up. Everyone seemed a bit anxious. Jackson gave Javion a scathing look when he saw him paying too much attention to Rylea.

"What's wrong, Javion?" Terrill asked. "Are you nervous around a pretty girl?"

"Seriously Terrill. Come on man, stop playing around." Javion responded.

Jackson thought they were acting real immature. He kept a poker face. He secretly hoped Big Boy Parks wouldn't be in the park. The sun was disappearing behind untamed, green landscapes. Even though they crossed the park five days a week at roughly the same time of the day, it seemed later than usual.

The insects sang randomly and loudly. Crickets and night critters rattled off unfamiliar, tense vibrations. Nature in the park, stunted by thick pollution, reduced the wind current to a flow of stale humidity. The stench of filthy garbage spread throughout the park like the scent of fresh cut green grass on a warm summer day. As the boys moved deeper into the park, they became less talkative and more militant like, quieter and more focused as they moved swiftly past the area where they knew Big Boy Parks would be. Rylea, mimicking their behavior, chose not to speak too.

Their unity and strong energy force pulled

Rylea in like a human magnet. She paced herself effortlessly to keep up with the fellas. Their fast pace was united and determined. Larry's feet seemed to glide on air. The fellas all knew he was about to take off running. Javion grabbed Larry's arm and slowed him down.

"Sorry," Larry said. "I was trying to get a head start on Big Boy Parks."

"No matter what happens, Larry. We all have to make sure we get Rylea home safely. She's depending on us." Jackson scolded him.

"Okay," Larry said, biting the inside of his jaw while glancing over his shoulder.

"Whew-wee!" Several keen whistles sailed through the muggy air with strong implications. Jackson's skin tightened around his face. Larry immediately picked up speed.

Javion reached to grab Larry's shoulder, barely catching hold of his backpack strap. "Slow down, Larry, we don't want to scare Rylea. We can't run off and leave her," he whispered. Three to four steps further, Jackson pulled Larry out of flight mode again. "Settle down, man. We ain't scared of this punk," he assured Larry in an unfamiliar, arrogant bluff.

Jackson knew if they had to fight he would have to step up to Big Boy Parks, alone. For now, the giant in him had been awakened.

Chapter Ten

Intrusion At MLK Park

The sun dipped a little lower behind the evening sky. The array of red-orange and dark-blue colors from the sky reflected on the ground pushing their shadows further behind them. The boys were used to the many rustling sounds the park offered. But this time, the sound of suggestive whistling was in too close proximity of their walking path across the park. Then the sudden intrusion of a person screaming loudly broke the tension.

Everyone reacted to the yelling, including Big Boy Parks. The boys and Rylea scattered. Their feet moved fast away from Big Boy Parks. None of them looked at the others. Jackson carefully moved in on Rylea's left and Javion stepped to her right. Larry moved in behind Rylea while Terrill paced in front of her. Instantly they had formed a barrier of protection around her.

Rylea never felt so secure walking through the park or anywhere else that she could recall. The protective barrier formed around her, by the boys, gave her a sense of security and calmness. Rylea felt empowered by the boys' bond to protect her from potential danger. She had not felt so protected since she was a little girl, before her dad left them. The unsteadiness of moving from place to place along with her parents' divorce made her feel insecure. It was hard getting use to new kids. The boys, however, made it easy for her to interact with them.

Larry whispered quickly to Jackson, "I hear footsteps coming up fast behind us." Focused on protecting Rylea, Jackson didn't hear Larry's warning.

"Run, run," Larry shouted suddenly. The moment he said, "run", his long legs were already suspended in mid-air.

"Rylea, let go of your backpack," Jackson demanded firmly. He quickly slipped the weighted pink and white backpack from her back. Free of the backpack, she glided through the park. The others ran as fast as they could. Rylea's legs were like those of a young gazelle, lengthy and beautiful making long strides across the park. She slowed down when she heard someone hollering again. The boys dropped their guard as well.

"HELP ME! HELP ME, SOMEBODY!"

Terrill noticed no one else was running. He stopped. "Somebody hollering for help," he stuttered through short-breaths.

"We can't go back," Jackson shouted urgently at them.

"Help me, Jackson!" the voice screamed even louder this time.

Jackson was torn over the need to protect Rylea and helping some stranger who obviously knew his name. Most of the kids at the middle school thought he had a bad reputation. But, he was seriously frightened by this person's cry for help. *Could this be a set-up?* He wondered suspiciously. *What if it's Big Boy Parks?* Jackson shook his head. *That doesn't make sense. He doesn't know my name.* Jackson's attempt to reason with himself was inadequate and deficient. He simply didn't have enough information to make logical sense of the situation.

"I have to go back to help the person," he muttered. His conscious wouldn't allow him to make excuses. Besides, he thought to himself, *What would Rylea think of me, if I didn't go back to help the person?*

"Help me!" More screams and pleas for help pressed through the muggy air toward the evening sunset. The urgent call rang louder in Jackson's ears. His father's voice of advice, *"Don't let them think you a punk, Junior,"* rang even louder in his head. In his heart, he felt obligated to go back. He knew his father wouldn't be so forgiving if he found out about the incident.

"Javion, you come with me," Jackson urged. "Terrill make sure you get Rylea home safely. Catch up with Larry, if you can," he demanded.

Jackson suspected Larry was probably on

the other side of the park, near the apartment building, waiting safely for them. However, he didn't want Rylea to think she was alone with Terrill.

Jackson and Javion picked up large sticks from the ground. They separated from each other. Playing and throwing the football in the park daily gave them a slight advantage. They knew each other's location. They could see someone lying on the ground hurt about a quarter mile back. The person had stopped yelling and was now not moving.

"Where da' police when you need 'em?" Jackson asked out of concern for the small, defenseless body lying on the ground. "What if he's dead?"

Jackson walked closer to the still body lying on the ground and stared down at it. He didn't know what to expect because he had never seen a dead body. *What would we tell the police, if the person was dead?* He wondered. *What if someone said I hurt the person?*

It was too late for him to turn around. It was also too risky to leave the person lying on the ground without trying to help. Meanwhile, he could hear Big Boy Parks in the background laughing out of control.

From Javion's position, he could see there was no one close to Jackson and the body. He didn't hear any more footsteps. He came out of hiding and stood alongside Jackson who was looking down on a small boy. Javion asked, "Is he dead?"

The evening sunset cast enough light between the trees and statues to where they could see that the limp body lying on the ground was one of their school mates.

"Aw man!" Javion said hysterically. "It's Lil Franklin! God, please don't let Lil Franklin be dead."

Chapter Eleven

Helping Lil Franklin

"Lil Franklin! Lil Franklin, what happened? Who did this to you?" Jackson demanded frantically while trying to pull Lil Franklin's half-pint body out of sight of the unknown predator.

"Jackson, be careful moving him in case something is broken," Javion warned.

As Jackson wrapped his arm around Lil Franklin to lift him, he could feel Lil Franklin's heart beating like a pair of African drums. His small hands trembled when he tried to wipe blood away from his eyes. His body relaxed, almost into a comatose state against the weight of Jackson's arm.

Jackson watched the thick, red blood oozing down the side of Lil Franklin's frightened, narrow face. He tried to figure out where the blood was coming from. There was so much of it, it was hard to tell. He was scared. He hoped the person that jumped Lil Franklin would not return. He had to get Lil Franklin out of harm's way. He was prepared to defend them by any means necessary.

"Help me! Please don't leave me here," Lil Franklin begged, trembling nervously. His voice trailed weakly.

"Since me and my mom moved into the neighborhood, I've been following y'all home every day from school. My mom lost her job and we lost our home," the boy explained. "I live in the apartment building down the street from where you live." Lil Franklin continued. "Lately a big boy comes out of nowhere and chases after me. Today, I couldn't outrun him. He wanted my backpack and insisted I give him money and food. I told him I didn't have nothing in my bag, but he didn't care. He called me a liar. After that, the big boy hit me on the side of my head and snatched my backpack off my back and took off running."

Jackson interrupted Lil Franklin, "Did you say a big boy?" Jackson and Javion looked uneasily at each other. "Can you tell us what he looks like? Does he have a big scar on his face?"

"I don't know. I only remember he was very big and hideous," Lil Franklin responded. "I'm scared. My address is taped inside the backpack. I know my momma will be upset with me for not learning it sooner. She told me to remember it and tear up the paper. That big boy knows where I live now. I'm so stupid," he declared. He started whimpering like a frightened child. He pushed his glasses up close to his eyes so he could see clearly. His shiny, swollen eyes dripped with tears.

Jackson had a mean streak, but it wasn't reserved for intentionally picking on people smaller than him. The person who hurt Lil Franklin had to be stupid and insensitive. He thought once more about his dad's advice, *"Don't pick on helpless people. They need help. Never fight a lost battle. Fighting someone smaller or weaker than yourself is like fighting a lost battle. It's inhumane and barbaric."*

"What kind of evil monster attacks a kid?" Jackson raised the question, thinking and feeling embarrassed about the way he *used* to bully other kids.

Jackson stared at Lil Franklin's helpless

body. He suspected Lil Franklin might have only weighed eighty pounds or so, and the eyeglasses on his face probably weighed three of those pounds. Lil Franklin was barely over four feet-eleven inches tall. The Puma athletic shoes on his feet looked like they were toddler size. Lil Franklin was smart. All his classmates liked him. Most of the kids at school looked out for him because they thought he was too weak to protect himself.

"My inhaler!" Lil Franklin remembered. "He took my inhaler! It was in my backpack."

"Your what?" Jackson frowned curiously. "Sorry, Lil Franklin, we don't have time to look for your toy."

"No Jackson. It's not a toy. I have asthma. I need my inhaler. It helps me breathe. Can we just look, please?" he begged. "Maybe it fell on the ground when the big boy snatched my bag. He swung me over there," he said, pointing left of where he now sat. "I was holding on to my backpack straps tight when the big boy grabbed me and yelled, "Gimme that bag on yo' back, fool." I tried to get away but he was too strong. That's when he threw me on the ground and bruised my arm and hand. Guys, please look around for the inhaler. I know we could be in danger, but my mom can't afford to buy me another one."

Jackson and Javion looked at each other. Jackson knew Javion was probably thinking the same thing he was, *lil* Franklin fought against someone probably four times his size. They haphazardly searched the area but Lil Franklin's inhaler was nowhere in sight.

"Well guys I can't afford to have an asthma attack," he stated flatly.

"We better get outta' here before that crazy

fool comes back," Javion said. "We don't know if he has a gun or other boys helping him. It could be a gang initiation for all we know. Lil Franklin, can you walk by yourself," he asked.

"I think so. It doesn't hurt too much," Lil Franklin acknowledged sadly. "I don't know what to tell my momma when I get home. She's already scared to live in this neighborhood."

"It's all right Lil Franklin. You don't have to tell your momma exactly what happened," Javion said.

"Yea, the last day of school is tomorrow and we only have a half day. It will be day light and you can walk home with us," Jackson said trying to sound optimistic.

Lil Franklin managed to feel better. The pain and discomfort seemed to slowly fade away with Jackson and Javion walking alongside him. If only he could tell his mommy about Jackson and Javion helping him. Lil Franklin was certain it would make her feel better, knowing someone was looking out for him, but for now, it would be hard enough to come up with a lie about his injuries. He knew it would make her sad to know or think he was being bullied again.

They helped Lil Franklin get across the park without further incident. They were relieved the big boy didn't show up while they were helping him. *Maybe the big boy was scared now since he saw Lil Franklin had someone to help him,* Jackson thought to himself. Jackson suspected he was probably hiding, watching them help Lil Franklin.

The apartment building was finally in sight. Now that they were close to home, Jackson felt much safer. At any moment, he could comfortably let his guard down. The streetlight buzzed, made a slow flicker and was his warning that it was time to go inside the apartment.

Lil Franklin thanked Jackson and Javion again. He bid them good night, promising to see them the next morning. Jackson felt good about their good deed. He knew they had to protect lil Franklin and Rylea.

Larry and Terrill saw Javion and Jackson walking with lil Franklin. They came out to the side walk and asked Jackson what happened to lil Franklin. Jackson told them the grim details about how the boy had fought to keep Big Boy Parks from taking his backpack.

"I guess we were lucky the scary fool didn't come after us," Jackson said. The boys all nodded their head in agreement with Jackson.

"Still, I think we need to be more careful and watch out for each other." Terrill said.

Jackson nodded his head to acknowledge Terrill's warning. He was barely paying attention though as he hoped Larry or Terrill would mention something - anything - about Rylea. For Jackson to ask about her would mean he liked her for himself. He didn't want the fellas to know he was interested in her as a girlfriend. However, he was curious to know if she said anything about him.

"What about Rylea?" Javion asked. "We can't protect no girl. Y'all know they can't run and then they start crying and hollering. I can't stand to see no girl cry," he complained.

Jackson quickly took to Rylea's defense. "What about Rylea? Did *she* cry?" He turned to Terrill. "Terrill, did she keep up when y'all was running to catch up with Larry," he asked matter-of-factly.

"Rylea is probably different than most girls we know," Larry said laughing heartily at Terrill. "Remember the rabbit and the turtle story. Rylea was the rabbit and Terrill was the turtle. End of story. She ran smooth past Terrill. She didn't look scared to me. If anything, she looked like Jackie Joyner Kersey running across that park."

The friends all shared another laugh at Terrill's expense. It was easier to laugh now that the threat of Big Boy Parks was gone. They high-fived each other and said good night.

Terrill didn't mind them teasing him at all. He could hardly wait to get to his room so he could sketch a drawing of Rylea's long, gazelle-like legs, stretched out running across MLK Park.

Larry ran into his apartment building. His

mother asked him what took him so long to get home and if he needed to share anything with her. He of course told her nothing was as important as putting his long legs under the table with his hungry belly, to eat her delicious food. She smiled and thanked him.

Chapter Twelve

Sleep Don't Come Easy

Jackson, hoping to bypass his father's criticism, quietly entered the apartment. His little sister rushed toward the doorway to greet him. She started bugging him to read her a bedtime story after dinner. Jackson quickly gave in to her. He knew she enjoyed the attention from her big brother.

After dinner, Jackson's little sister led him to her tiny box-like room filled with colorful dolls, teddy bears and miniature toys neatly displayed around a special play area. He sat on the side of the pink, brown and white princess bed, and opened the *Cinderella* book she gave to him to read. It was one of her favorite stories. Instead of reading the actual story, Jackson made up a factitious story about a boy-genius who fell in love with a pretty girl with red hair on Forest Street. He began reading, "They were friends, destined to be boyfriend and girlfriend."

His little sister smiled. "That's not a true story," she said laughing. "Jackson, you met a girl? Is she nice? Is she pretty, like me?" She asked repeatedly. Like his sister's excitement, he could hardly control his thinking about Rylea.

"No fair," Jackson replied. "You have to listen to the whole story first."

She giggled, showing two missing front teeth. Jackson appreciated her warm innocence. He turned the first page and continued telling the made-up story. Then he kissed her forehead. She looked fondly into his eyes, smiled and laid down on the small mattress. Jackson shifted the soft pillow underneath her head. She put her thumb in her mouth and prepared to listen to Jackson finish the bedtime story.

His heart was filled with love and he silently promised to always be there for her.

Jackson finished the made-up story about his and Rylea's life until his little sister fell into a deep sleep. "And they lived happily after," he said, closing the *Cinderella* storybook. He placed his sister's little body underneath the pink, brown and white princess blanket.

Jackson went back into the kitchen to look for after dinner snacks. He noticed his daddy still sitting in the living room, watching T.V. and holding an empty whiskey glass.

"Hey boy," he snarled in an irate tone, "you

better get yo' self in this house a l'il earlier. No more late nights out on the sidewalk hanging with your boys."

"Yeah. Okay. Pops." Jackson responded in a perfunctory manner.

"Don't try ta' get sassy with me boy. Um still yo' daddy," he further warned in a drunken slur.

Jackson remained unresponsive. He didn't want to provoke his dad or give his dad a reason to start complaining. He could sense when his dad had drunk too much liquor. His dad would literally sit in front of the TV watching the same re-runs for hours and hours, or pick a fight with him or his mom, for no reason. Jackson's only objective was to get cookies and milk to snack on while he thought about what it would be like going to high school with Rylea next school term. He wanted to get to know her over the summer months. However, his dad had other plans for him, to work.

"Good night Pops," Jackson said to his dad, slowly closing the bedroom door behind him. Jackson was sort of waiting for his dad to have the last word, but his dad had only one response.

"Night, Son. I mean what I said about coming in this house late."

After he showered, Jackson changed into his favorite, worn out superman pajama pants and an over-sized white tee shirt. He lay across his too-small twin size bed listening to several jazz artists reminiscing about Rylea until he drifted off to asleep. "Rylea," he whispered softly.

Rylea

Rylea had fallen asleep early. She was

exhausted from the run in the park along with getting up at five o'clock in the morning to help her mother with her little sister. She was glad she decided to ask Jackson about crossing the park with him. Maybe he wasn't as hard as some of the other girls said. *He seemed pretty nice to me*, she thought. She recalled how he protected her in the park. Although he tried to act tough in front of his friends, she was certain it was just a front.

Lil Franklin

Lil Franklin's mom was sitting impatiently on the front stoop smoking a cigarette waiting for him to come home.

"Hey mom. I'm home," he said, trying to project a big boy voice.

"Hey son," she responded. Considering other things in her life, she was just thankful he was home safely.

Lil Franklin was very grateful for the early dusk. And he was thankful he didn't need to use his house key to open the door. He was also thankful Jackson and Javion came back to help him. He eased by his mom, stepping slightly to the left of her so she wouldn't see the blood stains on his light-gray shirt, his bruised eye, or his scratched and swollen left hand. He knew she would surely be frightened for him. *I will worry about tomorrow when it gets here*, he thought to himself, concerned more about the fact that the big boy had his address and his house key.

Lil Franklin knew his mom would surely freak out about his injuries. Since losing her job and having to move, his mom had grown timid and easily disturbed over the smallest of things. Lil Franklin showered quickly, threw his torn, blood-stained clothes in the trash, and grabbed a prepared ham and cheese sandwich and orange juice from the fridge. "Goodnight," he said to his mom and went to his room to eat his sandwich while watching TV. He fell asleep watching a vampire movie.

Generally, Lil Franklin liked scary movies, but later he wished he had not watched the vampire movie. He woke up restless several times during the night, thinking he heard someone jingling keys in the front door. His heart thumped loudly, fearing the big boy was in his apartment. Lil Franklin peeped from underneath the covers wondering if the big boy had entered his home. He finally went back to sleep when he saw his mom checking on him. Lil Franklin hoped Jackson would help him get the house key back from the big boy that jumped him in the park.

Terrill

Terrill stayed up late. He couldn't sleep when he had an image on his mind. Terrill, similar to Jackson, kept his talent a secret as well. He often doodled and got good grades in art class, but his friends had no idea how good of an artist he was.

Before going to bed that night, Terrill had to get the image of Rylea out of his mind. He sketched a perfect drawing of Rylea's long, slightly bowed legs sprinting across the park. The sketch was drawn so skillfully, no one would have guessed she was running because she was afraid of some vile person in the park. Terrill cleverly personified himself as a tree root shadowed in the painting. He painted himself in the drawing implying the root to her beginning. Satisfied with the sketch, he fell asleep on the side of the bed, fully dressed in his clothes and shoes. Dark charcoal, used for the sketch, was still packed underneath his fingernails.

Traces of charcoal dust, left on his face, marked him a true artist.

Chapter Thirteen

The Last Day of School

It was early morning on the last day of school. The boys and Rylea only needed to cross the park one more time after this. They hurried through a slight fog, which had yet to lift from the park. The boys and Rylea walked quickly and quietly to the schoolyard. After they crossed Manchester Avenue to enter the schoolyard their defenses dropped. They didn't talk about the night before except to agree they would stay close together going home.

"We'll meet behind the gym again right after school," Jackson said. He intentionally looked at Lil Franklin and Rylea to make sure they understood the plan. Lil Franklin's face, was still black and blue from the fight in the park.

"We just need to get through school today," Javion encouraged them.

"You don't have to tell me twice. I'll be there," Lil Franklin said in a gentle tone.

"Me too," Rylea said. "I'll be there." She smiled warmly.

Jackson liked the way her beautiful smile slanted slightly to the right, revealing the small gap in her teeth, showing off her dimples.

"What about the movie? Are we on for the movie after school," Larry asked nonchalantly.

Meanwhile, all the other students were headed into the building toward their class.

"Jackson. Jackson wait up," Rylea called. She approached him and took his hand squeezing it gently. "I just wanted to say thank you for looking out for me yesterday."

"Yeah, we cool," he said. "See you behind the gym." Jackson couldn't lie, Rylea made him feel good. She made him feel human. In many ways, she was impeccable like the piano pitches in his head. He looked forward to seeing her in the hallway. He wished they had at least one class together, even though it might have made him feel awkward.

Jackson was anxious to get through this last day of classes. He didn't want to see Ms. Bell, but he had already committed to meeting with her before his gym class. There was no way to avoid her, knowing he had to practice with the band later. Jackson knew she was expecting him to at least top the performance from the day before.

The third hour finally came. All the choir and band students were in the gymnasium practicing. Chairs had been set up the night before along with the extra stationary instruments, podium, microphone, and recorders. Administrators worked on the sound check, while security personnel and custodians discussed safety measures.

Before long, parents filled the gym anticipating the end-of-year musical performance. The band and choral of students were arranged on the floor, excited to participate in the last of the school year performances. They were expected to perform five musical numbers, including both of the school's anthems.

Chapter Fourteen

La La Land

Everyone patiently waited in the gymnasium for the end-of-year musical performance. Ms. Bell walked in to view the audience, and they applauded immediately with excitement anticipating a *"bring down the house performance."*

Ms. Bell's reputation was unsung as she continued to reach new heights every year. Her gifts and talents brought in people from all over the community. School board members, city officials, the Mayor and other city leaders from nearby communities came to witness her performances.

Dressed for the occasion, Ms. Bell dazzled the crowd in a black, floor length gown glittering with rose-pink silver, and accessorized with a pair of Jimmy Choo rose-metallic opened-toe pumps. The fashionable, silver, palladium, dangling, tear-drop earrings and matching necklace and bracelet sparkled as she moved in front of the audience. On such a special occasion as this, she wore a classical, diamond ring, turned inward, that once belonged to her great-grandmother. Ms. Bell stepped with confidence onto the wooden, platform behind the podium. She turned to finally acknowledge and welcome the audience.

"Ladies, gentlemen, and students, prepare to hear the greatest band in the world. For your pleasure, we will perform five musical compositions, including both school anthems. As you know, some of the students have been playing for at least three years and some as little as a year. But I can promise this, you will hear the 'National Black Anthem' like you have never heard it before." The crowd applauded even louder. She waited for the applause to die down and then continued, "I encourage you to feast your ears on every instrument and sound we endow you with today. Thank you again for joining us. And, now, ladies and gentlemen…"

Ms. Bell turned to the nervous students, raised the baton and tapped two sequential sharp beats on the edge of the podium. The students, poised and uniformly dressed in black bottoms and white tops, came to full perfect attention. Ms. Bell smiled at the students, an indication for them to relax and smile for their parents, friends, and teachers in the audience.

She conducted the first two jazz musical compositions, an interpretation of Beethoven's classical, *'Moonlight Sonata'* and the traditional National Anthem, *'Star Spangled Banner'*. Then she prepared the students to perform the *'National Black Anthem'*. The audience listened intently, anticipating the best of the best from Ms. Bell.

Jackson and another student swept the audience with a sweet jazz pre-ensemble. The audience could not believe their ears. Not even a baby was crying in the audience.

Suddenly, the audience went wild as Ms. Bell took the audience by storm. In slow motion, she moved the baton into position, raising her left hand as if she were about to make a Cinderella wish. Her right hand was suspended in mid-air, now ready to conduct the most elegant rendition of the *'National Black Anthem'*. She looked toward the piano, directly into Jackson's eyes, and when he glanced back at her, she knew he was about to give a once in a lifetime performance. A pregnant pause seemed to float over the band members.

The audience appeared suspended in time anticipating a unique spin on the 'National Black Anthem'. Ms. Bell tapped the baton on the edge of the podium again, cueing the students to start.

Jackson knew he could not let her down, not this time. Even more important, he could not let himself down. This moment, this experience, this performance would validate his musical talents. It would say what he couldn't tell his friends. Jackson saw his mom and dad come through the door. His nerves were about to take over, and then he saw Rylea smiling, proudly. He had not done anything for her except to see her home safely.

Each group positioned their instruments. Ms. Bell cued the clarinet, flutes, horns, trombone, baritone, drum and lastly the piano. Jackson followed alongside on the keyboard. Ms. Bell, once again, raised the baton and the students played the beginning notes of the 'National Black Anthem'.

Parents, teachers, and students alike took immediate notice of the unorthodox sound that was being produced on the piano. The crowd, in surprise, riveted toward the boy on the piano who had the audacity to not just challenge their familiar way of hearing the song, but to uniquely play it at an incredible level that seduced their imaginations. They were awestruck with his ability to emulate the other instruments, meanwhile producing the anthem at an optimal level.

The very moment Jackson began keying notes, he escaped into a flawless, beautiful, familiar world where he'd learned to go when he needed to dig deeper to showcase his musical capacity. Musical notes burst forth from the piano in a way Ms. Bell never thought capable of a student. He made the notes dance as he played. Then Jackson stood from the piano bench, slowly walking the eighty-eight keys all in conjunction with the band playing. Not once did he miss a note or beat. His performance was nothing shy of legendary. The audience exploded with joyous energy and excitement.

The loud sound of the energetic clapping roused concerns from the principals, school security and other administrators. They rushed into the gymnasium, expecting to find something terrible. Instead, Jackson had ignited the audience into a staggering, hand clapping, feet stomping ovation!

The 'National Black Anthem' had never been presented in the manner in which he objectified the musical notes on the piano. Ms.

Bell made a wrist-cross with the baton signaling the end of the composition. Jackson returned from his internal world and rejoined the other members of the band. Ms. Bell turned to the audience and bowed proudly. Then she pointed to the band members.

The audience clapped wildly.

She pointed to Jackson, signaling him to stand and bow for the electrified, applauding audience. While he had been caught between two worlds, he never once heard the audience's excitement or the lively applauds for his music. However, in his interpretation of the 'National Black Anthem', finally, Jackson was seeing (and hearing) what he was capable of producing on the piano and how others responded to his playing.

His excitement was palpable. He felt invincible.

Parents and teachers approached to congratulate him on his début. Other people simply reached out to touch his hand or to pat him on the back hoping to get some of his electric energy. Many people gathered around trying to get close enough to say something or to take a picture with him.

Ms. Bell smiled as she watched Jackson feel the fire of being famous. The most popular girls from his class came up to congratulate him, but he only wanted Rylea's attention. He performed for her more than himself. She caused him to show sides of him he didn't know existed.

Rylea pressed through the crowd to stand beside him. His mother was simply speechless at the boldness of him to keep such creativity from her and his father. "Son," she said in a loving manner. "You play just like your great grandfather."

Jackson could tell his mother was immensely surprised at his musical capability. He also noticed Rylea there at his side. Her presence was both welcomed and undeniable.

The real truth came from seeing the prideful smile on his dad's face. "Son, that's a big responsibility you displayed on the piano today," he said proudly. "I hope you can appreciate how gifted you are." He pulled Jackson into a "father-son" hug and squeezed him tight.

Jackson was glad he could make his father feel something other than the alcohol he had been consuming. He felt like that fifth grader again, except he didn't feel the need to reject his father's advice any longer. It was as good as gold now.

Finally, Jackson strutted to where Ms. Bell

waited patiently for him. "See? I told you so," she said with a smile on her face. "Ms. Bell is never wrong about her students' gifts. Jackson, you are truly a gifted musician. I want to offer you free lessons on any musical instrument you would like to learn," she stated kindly.

She recognized he had a natural gift to play any musical instrument he desired. Like him, Ms. Bell remembered their fifth-grade conversation. Smiling awkwardly, she asked, "May I talk to your parents about how gifted you are, musically?"

Jackson nodded his head and held out his arm for a handshake. They shook hands like old friends calling a truce. He walked her over to where his parents stood and introduced her to them.

Ms. Bell, extended a business card. "Your son is incredibly gifted. I have enjoyed working with him and would love to continue. I've told Jackson that I would give him lessons on any instrument of his choosing, free of charge, with your permission of course."

Jackson's father, with unspoken appreciation, accepted the business card. Shyly he said to Ms. Bell, "You know, I used to play the same way. I wish someone had offered to take me under their wing. Thank you kindly, I'll have my wife get in contact with you to set-up the arrangements."

The students were excited over the performance as well as it being the last day of school. They were eager to go home and get their summer vacation started.

Students who walked home had already been dismissed to leave. Bus riders had either gotten on the bus to go home and those whose parents picked them up had left the building as well. Soon the gymnasium was empty of children, parents, and visitors.

The band helpers, custodians, and some teachers began moving music instruments and equipment back to the band room. Everyone was still in a state of elation, singing and dancing to the music inside their head.

Administrators, still in la la land about Jackson's performance, issued a much-appreciated announcement that flooded the hallways and classrooms, "Attention all teachers and staff. In light of the performance we just had, you may leave early today. You have the rest of the week and next week to clear your rooms."

Teachers and staff voices could be heard throughout the building yelling, "Thank you, Dr. Pearson."

For many of them the piano keys still rang with distinguishable clarity in their ears as they quietly sang the school's National Anthem and the "National Black Anthem".

Chapter Fifteen

Empathy for Big Boy

Jackson said, goodbye to his parents and, ran outside to meet the others behind the gym. They were discussing Jackson's performance and mimicking his behavior playing the piano.

"Man, I ain't never seen nobody play a piano the way you played today! How'd you learn to play with so much passion? Who knew you even had a piano to practice on," Javion commented.

Larry, acting like a news reporter, pretended to hold a microphone in his hand. He stepped to Jackson and interviewed him, "Mr.

Jackson, what a marvelous performance today. You offered such a captivating rendition of the *"National Black Anthem"*. The world wanna know a few things... Who is Jackson and who taught him to play so dog-gone good? And, wherever did you get the time to practice?"

Jackson spoke playfully, but proudly into the pretend microphone, "Well, Mr. Larry, I don't have a piano in my house – never did. But, when I hear a piece of music, I can easily replay it from memory without thinking about it. A teacher once said to me, 'Jackson, you got a real special gift for music'. I am embarrassed to repeat it, but basically this is what I told her, 'I ain't gon never amount to nothing but a thug.' Today, she proved me wrong." Jackson was relieved to finally share his musical talents with his friends and not be concerned with what they thought of him.

Caught up in how Jackson performed on the piano, they were all laughing and playing when the big boy suddenly appeared out of nowhere. He leaned in so close, Larry could see the boogers in the boy's nose. Obviously shocked by the immediate intrusion, Larry jumped back and gasped.

"Where y'all going?" The big boy asked boldly. He looked around at the group. Lil Franklin tried to wiggle his way between Javion and Jackson. Big Boy Parks held up Lil Franklin's backpack, "Is this yours, lil fella?" he asked sarcastically. "If you want it back you just gonna have to pay me for it. Give me twenty dollars and you can have it back," he told him.

Jackson felt his throat tighten with anger. "Hey dude. Give him his backpack!"

"Man, you live in this park – ain't no school

out here," Javion said. But it was to no avail, Javion staggered backwards from Big Boy Parks' body odor.

Jackson could tell the big boy wasn't bothered by Javion's bitter insult.

Larry warned him too, "Stop being stupid. We just kids. Where you think we got twenty dollars from? Our mommas and daddies ain't got no-money."

Big Boy Parks only laughed heartily at their small threats. Jackson had the impulse to jump the boy, but he thought it over before he did something he might regret. Rylea was there and he did not want her mixed up in their trouble.

Big Boy Parks turned toward Rylea making nasty, inappropriate remarks about her. Jackson's face became distorted. He clenched his fist and snarled his nose. His shoulders raised in defense like a cobra ready to strike its enemy. Fearless, Jackson stepped in Big Boy Parks' territory. They faced off head to head, shoulder-to-shoulder, eye-to-eye. Jackson could see the brown specks in Big Boy Park's stressed eyes and smell his funky breath. He too was caught off guard by Big Boys Parks' reeking body odor.

"I don't know what your problem is taking somebody else's stuff, bullying someone smaller than you and disrespecting girls," Jacskson said with anger. "You ain't nothin' but a big punk 'cause you pick on kids twice smaller than you and demean defenseless girls. Now, if you so bad, we can get this on like two big bullies and nobody wins, fighting like two fools over nothing. But I tell you this," Jackson said firmly, "I ain't planning on losing big boy. My boys' gon' help me kick your big, black butt. Or we can make a deal and both of us stop bullying," he stated, hoping to call a truce between them.

The adrenalize kicked in and Jackson was fiercely hyped. His surroundings momentarily went blank. The park was quiet of its noise and distractions.

"What you gon` do, Big Boy?" Jackson demanded through blind rage. His throat was so tight with anger, He felt like he was suffocating.

"Joey, Joey, get tha' hella-way from dem kids. I done told you about messing with other folks." An unseen woman yelled. Like Big Boy Parks, the woman appeared from out of nowhere. Brazen, young, but obviously aged by her circumstances, she yelled at the big boy.

The woman looked to be about five-feet tall, if she stood up straight. Her skin was similar to the big boy—weathered, dark, ashy, and, scaly. She wore dark blue gloves to cover her hands, an oversized, tattered, and a rust-colored polyester blazer. Although the weather didn't call for it, she wore a lightweight, green, flowery scarf, loosely fitted around her narrow neck. She yelled again, this time threatening his life in multiple, choice cuss words.

Big Boy Parks casually dropped Lil Franklin's backpack near Jackson's feet, and walked away complaining to his mother's backside, "Momma, why can't I have some friends? I want some friends I can play with too. When we gon' get a house to stay in like other people? I'm tired of living in this cold, stinky park," he complained sadly.

Lil Franklin quickly took the bag and looked inside for the piece of paper with his home address and the asthma medicine. Everything was still the same inside the backpack.

Jackson felt sad watching Big Boy Parks retreat back into the park like a wounded animal. He felt overly empathetic for the boy, knowing that the boy's circumstances were far worse than he could possibly imagine.

"Hey guys, maybe over the summer we can play a few football games in the park," Jackson said calmly. Everyone knew what he was thinking. "Sure," they said, agreeing with Jackson's intention to visit Big Boy Parks in the park over the summer.

Rylea extended her hand to Jackson, which he eagerly accepted. Then she smiled, her lips slightly slanted, revealing the small gap in her teeth and the appealing dimples on her narrow face. She knew what it was like to be judged unfairly. Rylea was very impressed with Jackson for attempting to reason with Big Boy Parks. She was glad that things hadn't gone too far. None of them could have ever guessed Big Boy Parks was acting out because he wanted friends and needed food and shelter.

Javion, interrupted abruptly, "How about we stop by Rylea and Lil Franklin's house to ask if they can go to the movies with us?"

Terrill took a football out of his backpack and began tossing it around.

Rylea rolled her eyes. "Boys," she said shaking her head. "They always have fun and can find anything to do to occupy themselves."

Epilogue

A Lesson Learned

Some kids may think it is okay taunt and tease, but is unhealthy for all involved. Jackson learned that there is always more to the story than most of us see right away.

Kids used to tease him about his size and they assumed he was a bully and that he was interested in sports, when neither was true.

Jackson and his friends made assumptions about Lil Franklin, Rylea and Big Boy Parks based on what they saw. However, once they took the time to get to know them, they learned they had been wrong. Lil Franklin was tougher than he looked, Rylea wasn't a scaredy-cat and could run fast for a girl, and Big Boy Parks wasn't such a mean bully after all!

Jackson and his friends were looking forward to the summer. They decided to take their money for the movie and buy some food and clothes for Big Boy Parks and his mother instead. It felt good knowing they were helping someone else.

Once thoughtful, but soft-spoken, the gentle giant in Jackson had been awakened. He embraced his size and his talent and looked forward to high school. He also looked forward to his musical lessons with Ms. Bell. Right before the end of year performance she'd spoken to him about his natural talent.

Jackson had been the tallest in elementary and middle school and undoubtedly that would be true for high school too. But now he would also be known as the "Giant Pianist", and for the first time in his life, Jackson didn't mind standing out above the crowd.

"High school, here I come!"

About the Author

Gail Cheatam

Born in Holly Grove, Arkansas, Gail Cheatam is an educator by trade, teaching within elementary, secondary and higher education. A life-long learner herself, Gail enjoys reading, writing, gardening and quilting.

The first-time author has a B.A. from MidAmerica Nazerene University, a M.S. from Kansas State University, and is currently completing a Master's of Divinity degree at Western Baptist College.

Married with five children, nine grandchildren and one great-grandchild, Gail enjoys spending time with her family and friends. She is an active member in her community serving on local boards and helps the underprivileged.

Eiffel Tower Books

Is an imprint of

The Butterfly Typeface Publishing

Your Story. Your Life. Your Words.

Contact us for all your publishing & writing needs!

Iris M Williams
PO Box 56193
Little Rock AR 72215
(501) 823 - 0574
www.butterflytypeface.com

"A life is not important

except in the impact it has on other lives."

– Jackie Robinson